The Way to Freedom!

The 'Motto' behind writing "The Way to Freedom!":

This story is written, based on the events that happen around me, around you and so around us. This is the story of every mother. This is very special and close to my heart. Because this is my anguish, anguish for so many days. Actually, this is the Anguish of every Indian Mother.

This book represents all the mothers and the pain of all the mothers of India. I wrote this story for a greater cause but not for applause. This is written based on my real-life observations and some true incidents which we all knew.

Therefore, I strongly decided that this has to be written, and this has to be told to the masses. And this should reach every Indian.

So, my dear friends, unite today and spread the word

up to the maximum. This book is dedicated to all the mothers

of India!

With Love,

Your Hemant Karicharla,

S/O Venkata Lakshmi Saroja.

PART I
THE PAIN

It's a Hanuman Temple. As it is not a Tuesday, there are very few devotees. A girl is standing in front of the god, closing her eyes and praying to him. She looks beautiful and innocent. Her face resembles the moon and her attire reflects our Indian tradition. In simpler words, it looks like a goddess standing in front of the god. Her name is 'Mahalakshmi.' Her parents call her 'Lakshmi' and her friends call her 'Maha.' Everyone likes her because of her pure heart.

But that day, she looks nervous. The priest observes her nervousness.

"Lakshmi! You are looking nervous today. Am I right? What's the problem?" the priest asked her.

"You know that my marriage will be there within a week. Everything went well till now. But I don't know, suddenly, some fear or some tension occupies me, as the day is coming nearer," she replied with a low tone.

The priest knows her very well; he knows that she is a child at heart. By understanding her problem, "It's natural, every girl experiences this fear. But after the marriage, once the love blossoms between wife and husband, everything gets changed. The love towards the husband and the responsibility towards the family will replace the fear. That's the magic around marital bonding," he explains to her in a caring way.

"And you are the girl with a pure and sacred heart. So, the god will surely give you a loving and caring husband," he adds.

By the time he said that, a married woman comes and rings the temple bell. Then he smiles and blesses her.

Finally, the day comes. The bride (Lakshmi) and bridegroom (Achyut) sit facing each other on the wedding stage, laying their hand on each other's head. They place a curtain between them. After sometime, the priest instructs them to remove the curtain. For the first time, Lakshmi sees him closely. Achyut is a tall and handsome guy with curly hair and a broad forehead. Everyone is praising the lovely pair. He looks straight into her eyes and smiles gently. Then she bends her head down with shyness and then smiles.

***

CHAPTER 2: LIVING TOGETHER

On their First Night...

Achyut is sitting on the cot in the room and waiting for her wife, Lakshmi.

After a few minutes, Lakshmi enters the room, holding a glass of milk. She gives that glass to her husband. He drinks half of the milk and then Lakshmi drinks the remaining half. She sits beside her husband.

Achyut sees Lakshmi's face, and he realizes that she is feeling nervous. She doesn't speak a single word. So he realised and started the conversation to make her feel comfort…"Lakshmi, why are you so silent? Speak something," he asks her chivalrously.

"Can I ask you something?" she asks him in a low tone.

"Of course, Dear!"

"When you saw me for the first time in our house, you said immediately that you like me. What do you like in me?"

"While we were on our way to your house, everyone in the village constantly said, 'Our Lakshmi is so empathic, she respects everyone and she is beautiful outside. Whoever marries her will be a lucky man. From all their words, I understood that they love you and they have placed you not only in their family but also in their hearts. There I realised, really, how sweet you are and how lucky I'm, because I decided. Until there, I just came to see you. But from there, I came to your house, as I wanted to see you. Because I love you!" he tells her by seeing into her deep eyes.

He adds, "But from that moment, I was observing you. You are very nervous. I can understand the reason as well. Lakshmi, when you are with your parents, you used to be like

13

a kid. I like the kid in you. If you are to be with me in the same way, I'll be happier, in fact I love it!".

Lakshmi listens to all his words. Then she hugs him and starts crying.

"Yes, I frightened and felt nervous until I entered this room. But now, after I spoke with you, they all disappeared. Except my mother, even I never held my father like the way I'm holding you now. I can't say anything more than this," Lakshmi cries with happiness.

Then tears roll out from Achyut's eyes. They are the tears of joy and happiness.

"I told you I love the kid in you, but you really became like a kid" he consoles her wife with love, wipes her tears and kisses her on the forehead.

***

The new couple moves into a new house. They arrange their belongings in an orderly manner in the rooms. Later, Lakshmi prepares food and Achyut helps her in cooking as they both get tired. After the food gets prepared, they eat together and till late night; they watch TV, then go to sleep.

On the next morning, they go to the Hanuman temple. By seeing the new couple, the priest welcomes them with a cheerful face.

The priest asks Lakshmi, "you are looking very happy and cheerful. It looks like all your fears are gone."

"It's all because of my caring and loving husband," Lakshmi replies proudly, looking at Achyut.

After the pooja, Lakshmi and Achyut sit on a bench in the premises of the temple.

"I've been coming to this temple for 20 years. Whenever I feel low, disappointed, or if I have any fears, then I come here and ask hanuman to help me overcome those fears. You know! He listens to all my rumbles, mumbles and complaints. He has always helped me all the time. I think he was tired of me coming to him often. To escape from me, he sent you into my life," Lakshmi explains her relationship with the temple to Achyut and smiles.

Then Achyut also smiles.

From the next day, their regular life starts. Lakshmi wakes up early in the morning and makes everything ready for her husband. Meanwhile, Achyut gets ready to go to his office by taking his lunch box, his wife prepares which.

In the evening, by the time Achyut returns home, Lakshmi arranges boiling water for him to bathe. After he freshens up, they both sit together and chit-chat, crack jokes on each other and laugh a lot. Sometimes, they share an intimate moment too. And then it's more often dinner time.

Going to the Hanuman temple was a weekly affair, else at least on weekends, they go out for movies, picnics and turn out every second of their lives cheerful. Day by day, their bonding strengthens. It just feels like Love is in the air.

Few Days Later;

On one evening, Lakshmi suddenly feels dizzy and is about to faint. Then Achyut rushes her to the hospital. There a doctor examines her and informs them they will become parents soon. Achyut and Lakshmi heard the news, and he felt like there are no limits to their happiness. They felt like they were in seventh heaven!!

***

From that day, Achyut looks after his wife with additional care and treats her like a newly born baby. He frequently monitors her health condition. By keeping their family doctor's advice in mind, he puts all his efforts to make her things get done and arrange everything she wants on time. Lakshmi's mother has no enough strength to look after her, so she visits her now and then and stays along with her for 3-4 days in a week.

As the months are passing one by one, her foot and legs get swollen sometimes, and she suffers from frequent fever and vomiting. During those critical times, Achyut takes leave from the office and is with her all the time to take care of her and he never lets his wife move without his support.

On one night, Achyut sits beside Lakshmi and he is brooding over something. Lakshmi observes him.

Lakshmi: "What are you thinking?"

Achyut: "While watching in movies, I can't realize anything. But now I understand as I'm watching you, how many difficulties a woman has to face, you are literally experiencing hell to give birth, how much pain you are suffering! Legs are getting swollen sometimes, suddenly you get vomiting, frequent fever, even it becomes hard to eat anything. Oh god! Not one or two. There are many. I can't see you like this, Lakshmi. I want to see you healthy and happy soon,". He expresses his anguish innocently.

Lakshmi: "Hey Achyut, please don't feel like that, I'm ok and I'll be fine soon. It's just 3 months from now. And you are always with me every second and taking care of me. So, you please don't worry dear. Even I can't see you feeling sad or looking dull," she explains to him with love.

Then Achyut slowly approaches her and kisses on her forehead.

***

3 months later…

In the Hospital;

Both the families sit in front of the operation theatre and they are feeling tense. Achyut is feeling even more tense.

A few moments later, the doctor comes out and tells Achyut that they are gifted with a baby girl and congratulates him. By listening to those words, everyone feels very happy.

Achyut enters the room curiously. He slowly takes his very small, newly born daughter into his hands carefully. As soon as he touches her, happy tears roll out from his eyes.

"She is looking cute and pretty just like you, thank you so much", Achyut tells Lakshmi with a cheerful face.

Lakshmi's face too is filled with joy and happiness. There are no boundaries for their happiness.

Achyut places the little kid carefully in the cradle and then goes near Lakshmi and sits beside her.

"How are you feeling now?" he asks her by caressing her hair. "All the pain I've been suffering since a few months vanished just in a second when I saw our baby, now I'm happy", she replies happily with a shivering tone.

***

CHAPTER 5: THE LITTLE PRINCESS

Hanuman Temple;

In the presence of two families, the priest is directing the First Feeding Ceremony (ANNAPRASHAN/Grain Initiation) for their baby girl, named as "Pragna."

First, Pragna's grandparents take a golden ring, dip it partially into a specially made semi-solid food and then feed it to the little baby by gently applying the food onto her lips. She cutely chews up the food that sticks to her tiny, delicate lips.

After that, they arrange Bhagavad-Gita, a pen, money and gold in front of the little girl.

Lakshmi standing at the other side and encouraging her to come and touch one of those things.

"Pragna, come on...come and choose one of these, my little kid..." Lakshmi is shouting with joy.

Then the baby slowly starts crawling towards her mother. Everyone there, looking curious, and the baby goes near them and touches the holy Bhagavad-Gita.

By seeing the little girl's act, everyone feels surprised.

"Your girl rejects the gold and money and holds the holy book. That means she knows what is valuable, she is a real gem, and she truly justifies her name PRAGNA," the priest praises the little girl.

Her parents feel proud and profoundly happy by listening to his words. Everyone is busy playing with the little girl.

In the meantime, the priest calls Achyut silently to a lonely place in the temple.

"Listen carefully; it's my responsibility to make you know everything regarding your baby. That's why I'm saying. According to Pragna's birth time, star and horoscope, we have to take utmost care of her at her age of '8'. After 8, everything will come under our control; she will reach greater heights. But during 8, we have to be more careful,' the priest tells Achyut.

"What are you telling swami? I can't understand..." Achyut expresses his fear.

"Hey Achyut! Nothing to worry, it's just a small negative period, I'm not telling to threaten you, I'm just saying to be careful, that's it. It's common to everyone's life. We have to overcome those minor hurdles with our self-confidence. If I say this to Lakshmi, she may worry too much and it's not good for her health. That's why I'm telling you secretly, keep it within you and just take some extra care during her 8th year, that's it, there is nothing more than that to think about it, understand," the priest explains everything to Achyut, besides stressing the point that he would be careful during Pragna's 8th year.

After the discussion, Achyut again joins them as usual, hiding his tension inside.

***

On that night...

In their house;

Lakshmi sleeps peacefully beside her baby. But Achyut keeps on thinking about the priest's words. He then wakes up at midnight and approaches near his baby.

Looking at her, "oh my little child, you are my god's gift, you are my little princess. You will grow stronger and stronger day by day and will lead a happy long life. No worries dear, I'm with you, I will be with you all the time, live the way you want, I'll protect you my princess. I'm not only your father but also your guardian, guide and a friend forever. Your Smile is my Strength, and from now on your happiness is my Aim. Be happy, god bless you my child, love you..." he whispers confidently and proudly near his girl's ears with the tears rolling down from his eyes and kisses her gently on her forehead.

***

Chapter 6: The Beauty of Motherhood

Lakshmi spends every second with her baby. Achyut, while he is in office, makes a call to the home every one hour and asks Lakshmi about his Little Princess, Pragna. Sometimes, Lakshmi keeps the phone near the baby, then Achyut listens to her cute voice while she is making a series of quick sounds with her tiny mouth.

Even at the evening times, he used to come early from the office to spend time with his child.

For the couple, the baby becomes their world. They always enjoy observing the innocent actions of her. Sometimes she shouts like anything, some other times she cries for the milk, she mumbles within herself and she uses to beat his dad on his chest with her tiny fist. But, in her every action, there is cuteness. Days are passing like minutes.

On one day, while she is playing in her mother's lap, she suddenly calls her mother "Maa…" by tapping on her chin with her little palm. By listening to that word from her baby, Lakshmi feels happy.

"Dear, did you hear how our baby called me now?" Lakshmi asks her husband with excitement.

"Yes, of course, I listened to it so many times Lakshmi," he replies with a smiling face.

"No, it's for the first time, she uttered the word so perfectly,", she emphasizes it with more excitement.

"You don't know exactly how happy I'm now and I'm experiencing a strange feeling, I can't explain it," she expresses her joy to him.

At that very moment, Pragna again calls her "Maa….

Maa…. Ma…. Maa…. Amma…" continuously by tapping on

her cheeks. Lakshmi's eyes fill with happy tears.

She is enjoying the greatest moment of her life. One

can't define her happiness, the happiness of being a mother. It's

more worthy than any other thing in the universe.

***

That evening, they go to the Hanuman Temple.

Lakshmi shares her happiness with the priest.

By listening to her words, the priest tells her like this…

"Lakshmi, do you know why the children utter 'Maa' as their

first word? I'll tell you. We treat children as equivalent to god.

And they utter 'Maa' as their first word. That means, it is to

make us remind every time that Maa is the origin of this entire

Universe.

29

"As the time comes, I'm saying to you another important thing, listen carefully! Now, your birth has given a fulfilment to your life Lakshmi. I'll explain to you, in a simpler way, how. A girl can secure 25 marks during her birth itself. At the moment she wears the 'Mangala-Sutra' (when she got married to her soulmate), she gets another 25 marks. But, when she gives birth to a child, she secures the remaining 50 marks and her birth attains completeness.

"To become a mother, makes a woman complete. That's the greatness of Motherhood. Now, you received that honour in your life. And from now, your responsibility is to achieve its eternity by protecting your child and transforming her as a symbol of purity and honesty," he explains.

The words of the priest fill the joy and boosts up the confidence in Lakshmi.

"Yes, I'm there for her. Every second of my life is for my little princess. I dedicate my life to my baby and my husband," she says with a tone of happiness blended with confidence.

"And you know that Pragna's birthday is next week, so we decided to celebrate her first birthday here with your blessings and in the presence of my Hanuman " she adds.

"I remember my child; Let's celebrate the festival here grandly among and along with the blessings of Bhakta Jana (devotees)", he replies with a smiling face.

***

CHAPTER 7: PRAGNA

Hanuman Temple;

On that day, the temple is completely decorated with Arches that are made with green leaves and beautiful flowers. Apart from their family and friends, so many devotees come there to bless their little princess, Pragna.

It looks like a festival. Extravaganza spreads everywhere in the temple. Among all their cheerful faces, Achyut and Lakshmi enter the temple along with Pragna.

Pragna lit the temple with her bright face. After the priest performs pooja to the Lord Hanuman, Lakshmi and her companions make a special sweet and offer it to the god as NAIVEDHYAM. Later, Lakshmi feeds the sweet to Pragna and distributes to all the devotees there.

After that, a Haridas comes there, he who uses to narrate stories and tales related to Ithihasa and some moral stories through a traditional style of singing. As that is Pragna's birthday, he narrates "Panchatantra Tales".

Later, it is followed by a Mass Feast. Everyone who came there blessed Pragna heart fully. In that way, Pragna's first birthday was celebrated grandly like a festival.

***

From the next day, they resume their routine lives. But their love towards their daughter increases day by day.

Pragna starts walking cautiously by taking the support of walls, she sometimes falls on the floor, gets up herself and tries to stand erect again by applying huge efforts.

When every time the little girl does it, Lakshmi observes her with great joy. If she gets hurt even a little, the mother suffers a greater pain.

33

Starting with the word Maa, the little baby continues to learn new words daily, some unknowingly and some through the prompting given by her mother.

Achyut buys a new camera to capture beautiful moments of his child. We can't define their happiness, their love, which is unconditional and endless.

In that way, they too become like small kids and do all the naughty things to make her smile and laugh all the time. The time dissolves quickly and by the time they realize, Pragna enters the 4th year.

***

Achyut and Lakshmi take Pragna to BASARA SARASWATHI DEVI TEMPLE to attain Saraswathi Matha blessings for their child to start her education.

After returning to his hometown, he starts his search for a better school for Pragna.

34

Finally, he finds one school, and he joins Pragna there.

Pragna grasps everything quickly and she utters tough words easily with minimal efforts and she always stands as the unique one among all other children of her age.

She surprises her teachers, parents and the neighbours every time with her sharp Intelligence. Everyone loves her, as she is such an adorable soul.

Achyut fixes the beautiful photographs of his daughter on the wall of the Living Room, which were captured at her different ages starting from 1.

On one evening;

Pragna is cutting her 8th birthday cake in the presence of his friends, neighbours and parents. At that moment, all the children who gathered there are counting numbers "1, 2, 3, 4, 5, 6, 7, 8….", denoting that she enters the 8th year.

By listening to that, Achyut suddenly remembers the words of the priest, the caution.

Then he immediately goes into the bedroom. He feels so nervous.

"okay, from now we have to be very cautious and conscious about Pragna. If we do that, nothing will happen. Then there is no need of getting nervous," he tells himself and gets back to normal.

***

On one day…

Phone rings in their home. Lakshmi lifts it. It is from the school.

"Good morning mam, we are calling from Saraswathi Global Schools. Today, you didn't send Pragna to the school right. May I know the reason mam? Because the half-yearly examinations are nearing," the caller says from the other side.

36

By hearing that Lakshmi gets shocked!!!

"No, we have sent her. My husband dropped her in the school. Can you please check from your side once?" Lakshmi requests her with a shivering tone.

"Ok mam, we will check again and let you know," she says and ends the call.

But Lakshmi feels nervous and frightened and hence she decides to go to the school directly to check whether her Pragna is there or not. Immediately, she leaves the home and starts her journey to the school.

***

Lakshmi reaches the school and enters it. She approaches the receptionist and mentions Pragna's name there.

"We are sorry mam, she is there. It is all because of the wrongly taken attendance, a small confusion," receptionist explains to her the situation.

"How can you say like that, it is not at all a small thing! Do you know how the parents react to such things? I literally quivered with fear," Lakshmi shouts at her with a shivering tone.

Meanwhile, Pragna comes near her mother. By seeing her daughter, she immediately hugs her and starts crying, she kisses her all over her face.

"Why are you crying, Maa?" Pragna asks her mother in a low tone.

"No dear, I'm not crying," she replies by wiping her tears and smiles.

At that moment, Lakshmi can't leave her daughter there. So, she takes her daughter along with her to the home.

***

On that evening…

Achyut comes home from the office. Pragna runs towards her father with joy. He gives his bag to his wife and takes Pragna into his hands.

His tired face becomes bright again on seeing her daughter's smiling face.

"Daddy, today I came home very early, Maa came and brought me to the home in the morning," Pragna tells everything to her father.

"Why, what happened?" he questions Lakshmi.

Lakshmi explains to him what had happened in the morning.

After a few seconds of silence…

Achyut: "You didn't tell me this till now! You should have called me!"

Lakshmi: "I thought you were busy, and I could not think properly because of nervousness."

Achyut: "That's what my intention is. You may not be able to handle such situations every time. So, it is better to take my help. And I don't want you to take the risk. And I don't want to take a chance regarding our daughter. Lakshmi, we should be very careful, very. Even if it is a mistake of others, but ultimately that makes our daughter suffer. So, we must take care about every minute thing. Lakshmi, nothing is important to me than both of you. I don't want my family to get disturbed, even for small things. That's all I want to say, Lakshmi," he expresses his anguish to his wife.

Lakshmi: "I know, dear, how much you love us. I promise you, from now on I'll tell you immediately, if anything happens. But nothing will happen, because Hanuman always protects us," she tells her husband with a smile.

Then, Achyut also smiles and kisses his wife and daughter. Later, Achyut gets fresh up and they have their dinner together.

***

From the next day, the school management takes extra care regarding Pragna. Achyut also used to make a phone call every evening after Lakshmi brings her daughter home. And he strikes off every day in the calendar and counts the remaining months in the year.

As the days are passing, on one day, they come to know that Lakshmi will give birth to another baby.

***

CHAPTER 8: SHE WENT MISSING!

That is Sunday…

Pragna is sitting in the veranda and colouring pictures in her drawing book. Lakshmi closes the gates and warns Pragna not to go anywhere without telling her and goes into the kitchen.

After a while, Lakshmi's mother comes to their home and enters directly into the kitchen. By seeing her, Lakshmi feels happy and calls her husband with joy. Then Achyut comes out of his room to greet his Aunt. Then Lakshmi's mother asks them about her granddaughter.

"Haven't you seen her? She is in the veranda," Lakshmi tells her mother.

"Veranda! If she is there, why did I ask you?" she replies.

By listening to it, Achyut suddenly goes to the Veranda and comes to know that Pragna is not there.

"You both search in the home, I'll go out and search the nearby roads," Achyut instructs them and runs out and starts searching for Pragna.

He screams her name wherever he goes, but he doesn't get any response from her. After searching on the roads for some time, he returns to the home.

"Do you find her?" they ask Achyut with curiosity on seeing him.

"No, she is not there within our surroundings," he replies with weariness.

"Even we searched every inch and every corner in the home, but no use," they tell him with worried tones.

Tension prevails in their house. Achyut's heart beat faster. All the three turned to stone and remained with no clue!

44

***

45

Achyut tries to control the tension rising within him and starts thinking. He observes the veranda carefully and notices a stool placed near the gate.

On seeing that, "Lakshmi, did you put the bolt at the top of the gate," he questions his wife.

"Yes, I did," she replies.

"Hm, look at the stool. She unlocks the bolt by climbing it. That means something had strongly attracted her and made her leave the house," he concludes based on his observation.

"But what made her do so?" he raises the question again.

Lakshmi starts thinking. After a moment of silence, "Ice-Cream," she blurts with a curious voice.

"Yes, every time she runs after the Ice cream whenever it comes. Then I also run behind her to stop and bring her home. This is the regular phenomena which take place on every holiday," she adds.

By listening to that, Achyut runs into the home and takes his mobile and Bluetooth.

"Lakshmi you first make a conference call to all of our neighbours who are living within these surroundings, including me, and ask them whether any of them heard or see any ice cream cart," he instructs Lakshmi and starts immediately on his bike.

As Achyut says, Lakshmi makes the conference call to all her friends around and tells them what happened. All of Lakshmi's friends are trying to help her.

Achyut goes to the place where all the colony nodes meet and stops the bike there.

As all of them start speaking at once, he cannot understand even a word.

"Wait, wait, wait…. please speak one by one. Then I can understand what you are saying. OK, if anyone of you sees any ice cream cart moving in front of your house, or you hear its noise, then you speak up first," he instructs them.

To his question, a woman answers: "Achyut, I did not see the cart, but I heard the cart which was going ten minutes ago!"

"Really! What is the number of your road, mother?" he asks her.

Then she says that it is road number 3.

Upon hearing that, he immediately goes to that road and meets her. Then she points out the direction where it went. Then Achyut goes according to her directions.

After reaching there, he inquires everyone about the ice cream cart. But to his disappointment, everyone says no.

At the same time, another woman from the call speaks: "Achyut, you don't worry. Every day, nearly by this time, an ice cream cart comes to our road. So, if it will come now, I'll inform you immediately," she says.

"No need, I'm coming to that road right now, then only I can catch him," he replies and reaches there on the bike.

Lakshmi is sitting at the entrance of the house and crying, her mother is trying to console her, the remaining people are standing outside of their houses and seeing whether any of the ice cream cart is coming on their way and Achyut is sitting on his bike and waiting for the ice cream cart.

After a while, breaking the silence, a man enters the road with his ice cream cart. On seeing him, Achyut stands up and starts running towards him. Glaring at him, Achyut grabs his shirt forcefully and starts shouting at him.

"Come on tell me, where is the little girl, she is my daughter, where is she?" he asked him with a louder voice and furious face.

But he is so confused and frightened. "What sir, what are you talking about? I don't understand," he says innocently.

"Don't act bloody… those who saw you told me you only took my child with you," Achyut threatens him with a raising tone. Even though he doesn't know exactly, he just says like that to find out the truth.

But he continues to say NO. Then the people who are there also say that he is looking innocent and he is saying the truth. By listening to their words, Achyut leaves his shirt collar.

Achyut: "Sorry brother, I'm worrying about my daughter, that's why I behaved like that, I'm sorry!"

That guy: "It's OK, I understand!"

Achyut: "OK, do you know who else is selling ice cream in this area, other than you?"

That guy: "Yeah, there are two more guys who sell ice cream in this area."

Achyut: "Then can you please tell me where they can be by this time?"

That guy: "I don't know exactly, but I know the area where they are living."

Achyut: "Oh! Very good, then please take me to their area right now."

That guy: "But… my cart...?"

Achyut: "You please don't worry about your cart, they will take care of it, you please come with me, please…"

That guy: "Okay! Come on, I'll take you there!"

Achyut: "Thank you so much, brother. Lakshmi, I'm going to the police station, I'll file a complaint there and I'll go to their area along with the policeman. You just take care of yourself and don't leave the house!"

Lakshmi: "OK, Achyut!" she says with a shivering tone.

Achyut: "Oh! Lakshmi, you please don't cry, I'll return to home along with our daughter, so you please be brave," he tells her and tries to console her.

Then Achyut and the ice cream vendor start immediately on that night to search Pragna in the light of hope.

***

CHAPTER 10: NO MERCY!

Achyut goes to the Police station along with the ice-cream vendor. The sub-inspector, Narasimha Rao and Achyut were the college mates. So, he receives Achyut well. Then Achyut narrates to him how his daughter went missing and all his attempts to find her. Narasimha Rao listens to every detail carefully.

Narasimha: "Based on your explanation, me too assuming that the primary suspect is one among those two ice-cream vendors. So, now we have to confirm whether they are only suspects or the culprits. But if I come like this, they won't reveal their true faces!"

By saying that, Narasimha changes his dress and all the three along with a head constable start in a jeep towards the place where the suspects living.

***

While they are on the way…

Narasimha: "If, in case, what we are thinking is right, then any of them might belong to any child trafficking or any kidnapping gang."

On listening to that, Achyut feels very nervous. Narasimha observes that.

Narasimha: "Hey! Achyut, you don't worry. These are all just assumptions and you, with your presence of mind, found the place where they are staying. We will definitely find your daughter within an hour. That's my promise!"

***

Ice-cream vendor: "Sir, that is their area and those two are their houses," he tells by pointing out two small houses which are at some distance from them.

Narasimha stops the jeep there itself and they move towards their houses. They stop at a bakery which is right in front of their houses. Inspector takes one cigarette, Achyut takes a water bottle, and the constable takes a curry puff.

Then one suspect comes to his home, on seeing him, his children come to him cheerfully. He gives them some snacks and they take them curiously. He also brings few vegetables and gives them to his wife. After that, he plays with his children outside.

After a while, another suspect also reaches his home. Then he immediately starts drinking alcohol and beating his wife and children for every little thing with no reason.

By observing the two suspects, "He is the one who kidnapped your daughter. See how he behaves with his kids and wife with no mercy," the inspector concludes.

With no delay, Narasimha goes and holds the collar of him and drags him forcefully.

Narasimha: "Move, you bastard, you are under arrest!"

Suspect's wife: "What happened, sir? Why are you taking my husband?"

Narasimha: "Your husband kidnapped a girl; we have all the evidence", he tells her with an angry tone and she is shocked.

In the meantime, he tries to escape from him, but Achyut immediately catches him.

Narasimha locks his hands with cuffs. The first ice-cream vendor goes to his home. Then Narasimha, Achyut and the head constable start from there in the jeep along with the suspect.

***

It takes so much time to reach the police station from there. So, Narasimha stops the jeep at a deserted place. He then beats him.

Narasimha: "Where is the girl?", he asks the same question repeatedly.

Then suddenly, he shouts at them and says, "I killed her".

Everyone gets shocked on listening to that. Achyut turned to stone. A horrible silence occupies over there.

Breaking that silence, Inspector speaks…

Narasimha: "You bloody, tell me the truth. If you tell the truth, then I'll reduce the punishment. Otherwise I'll kill you here itself!".

The Culprit: "Sir, I'm already caught and what do I get if I tell lies?"

Narasimha: "Oh, alright! Then show me the proofs."

The Culprit: "Come with me, I'll show you right now!"

They again start in the jeep and go according to his directions.

***

Here at Achyut's house, Lakshmi, her mother and some of her neighbours are waiting for Pragna and Achyut. Lakshmi keeps on crying.

Lakshmi's mother: "Lakshmi! You didn't take water even in the afternoon, and it is not good for you now as you are carrying. Please eat something."

But Lakshmi doesn't give her a reply even.

***

Finally, they reach another deserted place near to the Achyut's house. They get down from the jeep. That is a barren land surrounded with bushes and thorns. The fear in Achyut is increasing.

Narasimha: "Why you bring us here, did you hide the girl here?"

The Culprit: "Yes, I put her inside my ice-cream cart and brought her here and left her here."

Narasimha: "Where? Show me the exact place."

The Culprit: "I forgot! You search" he tells him negligently.

Then he and his constable start searching for the girl with the help of a cell torch. But Achyut doesn't move an inch from there. His face and total body get wet with sweat. He trembles with fear.

Suddenly, the constable shouts loudly on seeing Pragna in an unimaginable condition. Narasimha goes into that direction and he also gets shocked on seeing her. Her neck is bleeding, her dress got torn at some places, there are some nail marks on her body and blood stains are there on her dress below the abdomen. Body is there, but there is no life.

Achyut sees his lifeless daughter and starts crying. He cannot believe that bitter truth. He is suffering a deep pain in the heart. The pain is undefined and unending.

Suddenly, he remembers Lakshmi. He can't even imagine how she will react. He is not brave enough to take his daughter to his wife.

Finally, inspector Narasimha and constable make him move and take him to his house along with Pragna.

***

On seeing his husband along with her daughter in his hands, Lakshmi stands with a cheerful face and goes near Achyut to see her child.

Lakshmi: "Oh my dear Pragna! You finally came home, I'm very happy!"

She tries to take her into her hands, but Achyut denies giving her.

Lakshmi: "Give her to me Achyut, I have to feed her food now. Is she sleeping? And why are you still looking dull?" she asks her husband and takes her child into her hands.

When she touches her, she realizes that her little girl lost her life. Lakshmi turns dumb. Even though the truth is visible in front of her eyes, she is thinking her eyes are deceiving her.

A wild act of a demon leaves a great misery to them and pushes them into a deep ocean of sorrow. The little girl didn't even know what he did to her. She ran after him with an

innocent face, but he treated her with no mercy.

***

The ice-cream vendor is sentenced to death.

Achyut is coming out of the court...

Media surrounds him...

Reporter: "Sir, the offender was punished, but none can compensate for your loss. On this account, do you want to express anything to the people?"

After some silence...

Achyut: "He did a crime, a sin, so he was punished. But what did my Pragna do? What did we do? Why are we punished? Even death itself is no bigger than this.

"She was a brilliant girl, she always surprised us with her Intelligence, she was always cheerful, kind, she loved everyone and everyone loved her. If she were alive, she would have been a pride of the society. We missed her. And the entire nation missed a gem because of the wild act of that demon!" Achyut expressed his anguish with a shivering tone.

Another Reporter: "What you say to the parents of every girl?"

Achyut: "My wife is pregnant now. She has been carrying for 8 months. She expressed her fear that what would be the situation if another girl child will born.

"But I'm praying to god to give me a girl child again. If that happens, I believe my Pragna is born again. We took great care of her, but we never taught her how to deal with such a situation. That means we protected her but not trained her. This time, I won't repeat the mistake, I will raise my child as a warrior more than a daughter and she will become the answer to all the questions that arise in the minds of girls and their parents!" He replies with a raising tone and he leaves.

A Reporter (facing the camera): "It looks like this is not the end and he will write a new inspiring story in the name of his daughter. I Hope this must happen and let us hope Pragna will be born again!"

By listening to his words, all the crowd near him shouts… "Pragna will be born again… Pragna will be born again… Pragna will be born again…"

Lakshmi watches all this on the television with tears rolling in her eyes.

Her inner voice: "That's the hope which keeps me still alive!"

***

End of Part I

***

PART II

65

THE SOLUTION

Behind every Hero, there is actually another hero who leads him to become successful! He is none other than 'FATHER'. Therefore, I dedicate this PART II to all the Fathers in India who strive unconditionally hard for their respective families!

- Hemanth Karicharla

CHAPTER 1

South Delhi; Night 9:10 PM. IST;

Deepthi Singh(23-year-old-woman) and her friend Mahendra Pratap Pandey(24-year-old-man) are returning home after watching 'Life of Pi' in Saket, South Delhi. They are walking on the street and discussing the movie. Finally, they reach a bus stop which is nearby.

***

Munirka (another street); 9:27 PM. IST;

They board a bus at Munirka for Dwaraka. There are only six others on the bus, including the driver. One of the men, who is a minor, has called for passengers telling them that the bus is going towards their destination. Suddenly, the bus deviated from its normal route, and it's doors shut.

By observing that Mahindra became suspicious, "Hey! Why did you change direction, stop the bus!" he objects?

One of them: "What you both are doing alone at such a late hour?" he asks in a wicked way.

Mahendra:"That's none of your business!", he replies angrily.

That Guy: "Then, we will do something with the girl now, so you please don't disturb our business", he laughs.

Then with the rising temper, Mahendra holds his collar, a scuffle ensues between Mahendra and the group of men. He is beaten, gagged and knocked unconscious with an iron rod.

The men then drag Deepthi to the rear of the bus. They beat her with a rod and rape her while the bus driver continues to drive. Deepthi attempts to fight off her assailants, she bites three of the attackers. But all her efforts are going in vain. She is shouting for help, but her voice cannot reach outside as they shut the doors.

Mahendra is unconscious and there is no one to help her. They brutally rape her and later they throw the both from the moving bus.

***

It is around 11 PM, a passer-by finds them on the road who are partially clothed. Then he immediately calls the Delhi Police.

After a few minutes, the police rush to the place and take the couple to Safdarjung Hospital.

Deepthi has given emergency treatment and they place her on mechanical ventilation. She is found with injury marks, including numerous bite marks, all over her body.

After a thorough examination, the doctors generate a report. "She suffered serious injuries to her abdomen, intestines and genitals because of the assault.", the report says.

***

Safdarjung Hospital, the next day (day 1 after the incident);

Deepthi is still on mechanical ventilation.

Speaking to the press, the chief doctor says, "her condition is very critical, she has severe injuries to her abdomen, they pulled her intestines out. And they used a blunt object for penetration which caused massive damage to her genitals, uterus and intestines."

***

Day 2;

With the help of CCTV at the highway, they trace the bus and find its driver, Shyam Singh. Police obtain sketches by taking the help of the male victim, Mahendra Pratap. Then they have found and arrested them. They include Shyam Singh, the bus driver, and his brother, Bhupesh Singh, who are both arrested in Rajasthan.

Vijay Sharma, an assistant gym instructor, and Pranav Gupta, a fruit seller, are both arrested in UP and Bihar. A seventeen-year-old teenager from Badaun, Uttar Pradesh, is arrested at the Anand Vihar Terminal in Delhi. Akshith Thakur, who had come to Delhi seeking employment, is arrested in Aurangabad.

***

Day 3;

Safdarjung Hospital: Deepthi undergoes her fifth surgery. Doctors remove most of her remaining intestine. After that surgery she becomes stable but yet critical.

***

Day 5;

Public protests take place in New Delhi at India Gate and Raisina Hill. Thousands of protesters clash with police and battle Rapid Action Force units. Demonstrators are baton charged, shot with water cannon and tear gas shells, and arrested.

Protests are rising throughout the country. Over 600 women belonging to various organisations demonstrate in Bangalore. Thousands of people march silently in Kolkata.

***

Day 9;

Safdarjung Hospital;

She is still in critical condition, and she is on the life support system. She is suffering from fever of 102 to 103 °F.

***

Day 10;

A cabinet meeting has held, and it is chaired by the Prime minister of India. In the meeting, they have decided to take her to Mount Elizabeth Hospital in Singapore for further care.

***

Day 11;

On the very next day, they all start along with Deepthi in an air ambulance to leave for Singapore. During the journey, Deepthi suddenly goes into a "near collapse". The doctors on the flight immediately create an arterial line to stabilise her, but she doesn't regain consciousness.

***

Day 12;

Mount Elizabeth Hospital, Singapore: Speaking to the media, the chief executive officer of Mount Elizabeth Hospital

73

says, "Her condition is extremely critical. She is suffering from brain damage, pneumonia, and abdominal infection, and she was fighting for her life."

***

Day 13;

Andhra Pradesh; A government hospital;

Early morning 2:10 AM. IST;

Lakshmi is admitted in the hospital as she is about to deliver. This time she is struggling a lot more than her previous delivery. Achyut and the remaining family members are standing outside the operation theatre and are feeling very nervous.

***

Mount Elizabeth Hospital, Singapore;

Deepthi's condition continues to deteriorate, and she finally leaves her last breath around 2:15 AM.

*****

At the same time, here, Lakshmi gives birth to a baby girl and in seconds difference, she gives birth to another baby girl too. To their surprise, she gives birth to two identical twins.

By seeing the two baby girls, Achyut realizes that this time, the god gave him double responsibility. He accepts the responsibility by taking the kids into his hands.

*****

A week Later…

Hanuman Temple, Evening 6 PM. IST;

Both Achyut and Lakshmi along with the kids in their hands stand in front of Lord Hanuman. After performing pooja, the priest comes near them and blesses them.

"There is a strong meaning behind every action of the god. He took away one child from you, but he gave back two instead of one. He just hid her somewhere for some time to make you aware of some things. The testing period is over. And to those who is mentally strong, he gives them immense responsibilities. Now, it's your turn to keep up the trust. God bless you." the priest says to them.

"In the past, I was just a father of a girl. But now, I'm a father of a great challenge. Challenge accepted and I can say that I'll become the father of the change. Yes, I'll raise them as a symbol of courage and as an ideal image for every girl. And it's not my promise, it's my only wish in my life.", Achyut expresses his views.

Priest: "The girl in the hands of Lakshmi is 'Pragna Punarvi' it's decided. Then, who is the girl in your hands? By which name, you want to call her?"

Achyut: "'S W E C H A', she is Swecha!"

Swecha is the kid who came out first and Pragna Punarvi is the kid who came out after Swecha. And another notable point here is, Pragna Punarvi has the same birthmark on her chin as the first Pragna had.

***

Until the duo reaches their 4th year, they live in the same old house. But after that, Achyut shifts them to a new house. The house is far away from the city which is located in an isolated place.

Lakshmi: "Why you choose this place Achyut, it looks deserted during mornings and scary during nights without street lights even."

Achyut: "Because of this fear, we once made a mistake. I want to raise my kids among tougher conditions and make them ready to face the toughest. Daily they should go to the school in the city from here, and should come home in the darkness without fear. They should know the difference between the light and dark, right and wrong, faith and myth. They should learn to be alone, to fight for the crowd and to be proud for the nation. I don't want to see them as a shining moon, I want to see each of them as a burning sun.", he replies in a raising tone, a tone of anguish, a tone of anger, a tone of confidence, a tone of fearlessness and that is a tone of an ambitious father.

Lakshmi astonishes by listening to his words and remains silent. That doesn't mean, she cannot speak against him. It means she obeys him, it's the silence that comes from trust and faith.

Meanwhile, Swecha and Pragna are playing on the bed.

Achyut: "Swecha, Pragna, come on, let us go out. Now the time has come to introduce the world to you both.", he calls them.

They both held their father's hands and went along with him to step into the real world of unreliability.

***

The two girls are enjoying the sight of the village. Till now, they have become accustomed to see the world from their mother's shoulders. But now, they are watching it individually.

Wondered by the beauty of nature, slowly, they leave their father's hands and start running over the green meadows. While their feet kiss the earth, the sun (rays) who is attracted by their cuteness, kisses their chubby cheeks and the cool breeze caresses their hair and hugs the curious kids.

Surprised by the sweet sound of their beautiful laughter, the birds come out of the nests and follow them. Sunflowers, amazed by their charisma, they turn toward those running roses rather than toward the sun.

After sometime, they get tired and look back and then realize that their father is not with them.

They look around them, but they find him no where. They hold their hands with fear. They call him out louder, but they don't get any response.

Slowly, the tension in their hearts grows. The grass beneath their feet pokes them like thorns. The sun strikes them hard with his hot rays. When they look around for help, the sunflowers turn their heads toward the sun. They feel isolated from the world and they start crying.

Suddenly, a shadow covers them like an umbrella, preventing the sun's rays from falling on them. Then they look back and stop crying by seeing their father.

Achyut gently wipes their tears and asks them why they are crying.

"Why did you leave us, where you went?" Pragna asks her father in a crying tone.

"You both, remember one thing, I may not always be with you, but I'm always there for you. Believe in me, but don't rely on me.", he replies lovingly and caringly.

Then they start going back home.

"See, enjoying nature is necessary, but understanding nature is compulsory. Learn to observe the things rather than just watching them. If you come out of the house, remember the way.", Achyut explains everything to them while they are on the way home.

Finally, they reach home. They get relaxed for sometime by sitting on the wooden bench outside. There is a short guava tree beside the bench. Swecha finds one fruit among the branches and asks her father to give it to her. Then Achyut shows her how to climb the tree and tells her to take the fruit by climbing the tree.

Swecha climbs the tree. On seeing it through the kitchen's window, Lakshmi comes out and approaches Achyut.

"What are you doing with them Achyut, at least give her support? You are simply standing like that. What if she falls down?" she questions him angrily.

"Lakshmi, I won't give support before she falls, but I give support while she is falling.", he replies.

"Oh god, but they are too little to learn such things.", she says.

Meanwhile, Swecha plucks the fruit, comes down carefully and shows it to her father proudly. He takes the fruit into his hands.

"I hope, now you understand, after a certain stage, age is not a constraint, it is just a number.", Achyut says to Lakshmi by showing the fruit.

By observing the truth in his words, she smiles gently and goes back to the kitchen.

Then Pragna approaches him and says "Daddy, tomorrow me and Swecha will go to the ground and come back home alone."

"Oh, really! That's my girl!", Achyut kisses Pragna with proud happiness.

***

CHAPTER 2

84

After a few weeks...

7:34 AM, at Achyut's house;

Achyut and Lakshmi are waiting for Pragna and Swecha who went for a morning walk. It is getting late when compared to usual timing. Lakshmi is nervous. After a few minutes, they finally come home. On the way, Swecha plucks a guava from the tree without climbing it.

Later, they go to school on their bicycles.

***

During the first period, the attender comes near their classroom.

Attender: "Excuse me sir", he calls the teacher.

Teacher: "Yes…"

Attender: "Principal sir is calling Swecha."

Teacher to Swecha:"Swecha, go!"

In the Principal room;

To the left side of the Principal, there is a boy and his father is sitting in front of the principal and Swecha is standing to the right side of the Principal.

Principal: "Swecha, did you slap Balu?"

Swecha: "Yes sir!"

Principal: "But why?"

Swecha: "He teased Aruna badly!"

Principal: "Then, give a complaint to me, you don't have any right to slap anyone!"

Swecha: "Well, if I complain to you, then you will give a complaint to his father, then what will he do? Will he slap him or hug him?"

Balu's Father: "Who are you to slap him?" he shouts at Swecha angrily.

Swecha: "I'm his classmate, his sister. Daily we pledge, 'India is my country, all Indians are my brothers and sisters…' Maybe your son forgot this, but I remember it always.

"If you punish him in your home, he will forget it soon. But, if he is punished in the crowd, he will remember it forever and get fear in doing such things in the future. Sir, you knew that I slapped him once, but you don't know how many times he misbehaved with Aruna and made her cry.

"Balu, you are feeling embarrassed even though I slapped you only once in the crowd. But you are teasing her daily in front of the same crowd, did you think at least once how it hurts her? I just did this to make you understand the pain.

"Balu, Schools and Colleges are like second home to us. We have to live together in peace and harmony, rather than with quarrels and disputes.

"Uncle, like boys, girls also come here to learn something and to achieve something. But what can we do, if you resist this little freedom of ours? You know one thing, Aruna has not been coming to the school for two days because of Balu's acts.", she explains everything to all the three.

All the three persons there listened to Swecha's words silently. They realize that what she said is true.

***

87

Later, the principal, Swecha, Balu and his father assemble at *Aruna's home*. Aruna and his parents are also standing there outside the house.

After a few seconds of silence…

Balu: "I'm so sorry Aruna, I promise you I won't repeat it again!"

Balu's Father: "So Aruna, from tomorrow you can come to school. And remember this uncle, if there is any problem, not only your parents but also I'll be there for you to help you.", he tells her by gently caressing her hair.

Swecha to Balu: "I'll tell you sorry tomorrow in front of all our classmates.", she smiles.

Everyone feels very happy there. Meanwhile, the Principal looks at Swecha proudly.

***

On the next day in the school;

Balu says sorry again to Aruna in front of all their classmates and Swecha says sorry to Balu. The entire classroom fills with a friendly and lovely atmosphere.

In the meantime, the Principal came into the class. On seeing him, everyone in the class gets quiet and sits in their respective places. Then he calls Swecha onto the dais.

Principal: "Dear Students, you will go to the colleges within a few months. Which means, you are almost grown up and you are no longer kids. So, try to behave like a complete man or a woman rather than as a small boy or girl.

"See, you have to learn many things from Swecha like positive thinking, bravery, attitude and many more. Swecha, you have all the qualities to be a leader. I wish you all the best, god bless you", he appreciates Swecha.

Swecha: "Thank you sir!" she smiles.

***

After school, on their way home…

Pragna finds an old woman begging on the street. Then she stops the bicycle and goes near the old woman. She looks sick and weak with a torn saree. Pragna buys a bun from a nearby bakery and offers it to the old woman. But she just sits like a rock with no reaction. Then Pragna holds her hand and realizes that she is suffering from high fever.

Meanwhile, Swecha comes there.

Pragna to Swecha: "Oh my god! She is suffering from high fever and she is not even in a position to take food. What to do?"

Swecha: "Okay… You do one thing. Take her to the hospital and admit her there. I'll go home and come to the hospital along with dad.", she suggests.

Pragna: "Okay!"

Swecha starts on a bicycle to home and Pragna along with the old woman starts in an auto to the hospital.

While Swecha on her way to home…

It is getting nearly dark. A thorn belt is placed on the road on her way to home. As she is in a hurry, she fails to notice it. She rides her bicycle on it then both the tyres get punctured. She gets down from the bicycle and notices the thorn belt. She then understands that someone intentionally placed it there.

At that moment, a shadow appears beside her shadow. On seeing it, she suddenly turns back. Then someone runs fast and hides behind a tree.

She then slowly approaches the tree, but surprisingly there is no one at the tree. Then she immediately looks around with her sharp eyes but the place is empty.

So, she goes back to the place where her bicycle got punctured. But her bicycle is not there. She slowly goes near the thorn belt. Again, the shadow appears there. Swecha sees it.

Swecha to the shadow:"Okay, I understand. You are expecting something from me. But now, I have no time. I have to save an old woman. So, my dear bold man, keep my bicycle with you, I'll collect it from you tomorrow.", she shouts at the shadow and runs from there.

***

Swecha finally reaches home. By the time she reaches home, Achyut is removing his shoes as he just came from the office. Swecha tells her father about the old woman and then they both start from their home to the hospital.

In the hospital, 7:30 PM;

The old woman is placed in an emergency ward and they have given fluids to her through a pipe. Achyut pays for her treatment and medicines.

Swecha, Pragna and Achyut are sitting in the chairs outside the ward.

Pragna: "Sorry daddy for troubling you", she says with a low tone.

Achyut: "No Pragna, you did a wonderful job", he caresses her hair gently.

Pragna: "But daddy, she is very weak. Doctor said she has been without food for so many days and that if I didn't bring her here today, she would die tomorrow.", she says sadly.

Achyut: "It's okay dear! Now, everything will be alright and she will get well soon, you don't worry."

They spend some time over there and later go to their home.

***

Before locking the main door, Achyut has the habit of bringing both the bicycles inside the home. But he notices that there are no bicycles outside.

Then he approaches his daughters and asks them about bicycles.

Pragna: "I left my bicycle at the bakery uncle's shop and told him I'll collect it tomorrow."

Swecha: "My bicycle got punctured. So, I left my bicycle at the puncture shop and came home on foot."

Achyut: "So, I have to drop both of you tomorrow. Okay, good night, girls."

Swecha and Pragna: "Good night Dad!"

***

Pragna goes to sleep while she is thinking about the old woman. But Swecha remains unsleepy and thinks about the other shadow.

***

Next day morning;

Achyut takes his daughters to school on his bike. While on their way, Swecha is keenly observing the place where she was stopped by the stranger the previous day. But there was no one at that time.

They enter the town, and Achyut stops the bike at the bakery shop. The puncture shop next to the bakery remains closed.

Achyut: "They didn't open the puncture shop yet, what to do?"

Swecha: "It's okay dad, we will go to school on one bicycle. I'll take my bicycle in the evening"

Achyut: "Good, that's fine!"

Pragna: "Dad, please come early in the evening, we have to go to hospital to see her."

Achyut: "Sure, my baby, see you in the evening, take care girls.", he says to them and goes to the office.

Pragna and Swecha:"Bye Dad"

Then Pragna and Swecha reach the school on one bicycle.

***

On that day, during the classes, Swecha continues to think about the stranger. Pragna notices Swecha's unusual behaviour.

***

During the lunch hour…

Pragna: "Swecha, what happened?"

Swecha: "What happened?"

Pragna: "That's what I'm asking, what happened to you. You are not here, you are thinking about something seriously, I noticed. What disturbs you dear.", she asks her caringly.

Swecha: "I met one stranger yesterday, near our ground in the village. He tried to trap me."

Pragna: "To trap you?! What did he do?" she exclaims.

Swecha: "He placed a thorn belt on the road and punctured my bicycle as I didn't notice it before. He then tried to scare me with his actions and he trickly took my bicycle from me. But here, the surprising thing is, when I told him I had to save an old woman, he left me.", she explained everything to Pragna.

Pragna: "He may have come for both of us. Well, whatever that may be, here the thing is that he knows everything about us. Maybe he is someone we know or someone who has been secretly following us for days. Because, without proper knowledge, he cannot do so."

Swecha: "Hm… We have no enemy. But his action reflects pure grudge. I don't understand who needs to take revenge on us."

Pragna: "Balu?"

Swecha: "No chance, the issue among us was resolved. So, there is no point of taking revenge"

Pragna: "Come on Swecha! I slapped him. But he thought, it was you. Principal called you and so you dealt with it without disclosing my name. Therefore, he targeted you. Don't you remember our Dad's words. Humans always have two faces. One is genuine which is mostly hidden and the other is fake which is shown to the world. So, in that case, we can't even believe Balu's father. And have you noticed one thing, Balu is not coming to the school for two days."

Swecha: "I didn't think in this way!"

Pragna: "Yeah, but all these are assumptions until and unless we unmask his face in the evening."

Swecha: "Yes, we have to be very careful and we should do this."

Pragna: "And let us win our first battle!"

***

After the school, Swecha and Pragna leave the school on their bicycle.

***

After a few minutes, they enter their village. Finally, they are about to reach the same place where Swecha met the stranger the previous day. They have seen Swecha's bicycle which is parked near a tree at some distance.

A man then comes from behind the tree and stands near the bicycle. Pragna, who is sitting at the back, takes two stones from her bag and throws them at him. But he narrowly escapes

99

from them. But soon she throws two more stones, then a stone hits his shoulders. Swecha continues to ride the bicycle faster and as she overtakes him, Pragna kicks him strongly on his back. Then he falls to the ground.

Then they immediately get off the bicycle and rush towards him. He tries to punch Swecha, but she escapes and Pragna gives him a blow on his stomach. In the meantime, Swecha holds his hands tight from behind him. Then Pragna tries to remove his scarf, but he strongly resists it with all his strength. Suddenly he crushes Swecha's toe with his hard shoe. Then she leaves him as she can't tolerate the pain. Then he punches Pragna and starts running.

Pragna tries to catch him. But she is unable to run, because her leg gets sprained during the fight and he finally escapes from them. All their efforts went in vain. They slowly reach their home with pain.

***

Upon arriving home, Swecha and Pragna immediately go to their room. Pragna cleanses the wound on Swecha's toe as her toe is slightly ruptured and later applies oil to it.

Meanwhile, Achyut comes home. Then Swecha and Pragna come out of their room. Achyut relaxes for a few minutes and later they go to the hospital to see the old woman.

***

They meet the old woman in the hospital. On seeing them, she bows to them by putting her hands together.

Pragna: "You have to bless us grandma", she smiles by holding her hands. She stands beside her bed.

Swecha: "How are you feeling now grandma?"

Old Woman:"Healthy, but not happy!", she replies in a disappointing tone.

Swecha: "What happened grandma?"

Old Woman: "Oh! I'm sorry, I shouldn't have said that."

Pragna: "Granny! Please tell us, what happened?"

Old Woman: "You saved my life. But many old people like me have died on the roads so far and there are many others who are about to die. There are many old age homes in the city, some charge money and a few are offering free services. But we don't know where they are. If you please don't mind, can you take me to any such old age home that offers free service, I'll tell the rest of the people which I know about it.", she pleaded with her.

Tears welled from the eyes of the two girls who heard her words.

Swecha: "Such a great heart! But why are you here? Is there no one to look after you?"

Old Woman:"We gave birth to the humans only, not to the sons and daughters. Because children who love their parents during their old age are gods.", she expresses her anguish to both of them.

After hearing her words, they both became very emotional. Afterwards, she slowly goes to sleep. Until then, Swecha and Pragna were sitting beside her. Later, they go to their home.

***

During the night...

Her words are recurring in their minds. They are lying on the bed and thinking about the old woman.

Pragna's inner voice: "Indeed, parents are gods. But she said that children who love their parents during their old age are gods. How mankind is so unkind! Her words reflect a deep pain. It is so unimaginable and unmeasurable!"

103

Swecha's inner voice: "No pain is greater than this! Those children who abandoned their parents are shameless. At this age, this suffering is more than a hell!"

***

The Next Day;

On that day, they go to the hospital along with their father instead of going to school. They take the old woman out of the hospital and ask her to take them to the rest of the old people who are suffering like her on the roads. Later, all of them collectively go to an old age home.

***

At the old age home;

The management of the old age home welcomes and admits all of them into their house. Besides that, they immediately call doctors and arrange emergency care for those in need.

104

Achyut and his daughters liked the way they were treating them and are very satisfied with their hospitality.

Before leaving the old age home...

Pragna: "Why don't you come with us granny?"

Swecha: "We love you grandma!"

Old Woman: "I love you too, my children. But I have to be with them. Because these are the people who stayed with me during my hard times. So, I can't leave them in the middle. I hope you understand.", she says to them, tapping on their shoulders.

"But god gave me two wonderful granddaughters and their grand love, I'm very happy now.", she says with a cheerful face.

Swecha and Pragna kiss on her cheeks.

Old Woman to Achyut: "I want to see the luckiest mother who gave birth to these precious gems. Bring her here once.", she asks him with a curious face.

Achyut: "Sure, my mother", he replies with a smile.

He looks at his daughters so proud and all the three leave the place with great satisfaction. Their hearts are filled with greater joy and love.

***

On that night, at their home; 10:30 PM. IST;

Achyut is doing some office work in the living room. Swecha wakes up and comes out of their room to drink some water.

Achyut: "What dear? Didn't you sleep yet?", he asks his daughter on seeing her.

Swecha: "I did, just now woke up to have some water."

106

Achyut: "Oh okay!", he smiles at her and resumes his work.

She then goes to the kitchen, drinks some water and while she is returning to their room, she notices a wound on her father's shoulder. Then immediately, 'the fight with the stranger' flashes in her mind.

Then she goes to her father and touches the wound. Achyut tries to hide it and deviate her. But he couldn't. Tears rolled out from her eyes.

Swecha: "I know, with no proper reason, you do nothing. We are extremely sorry dad; we didn't think that was you.", she says with a shivering tone.

Achyut: "Call your sister!"

Swecha awakens Pragna up. On seeing the wound on her father's shoulder Pragna too starts crying.

Achyut:"My dear girls! You don't have to cry. You have done nothing wrong. You don't even have to trust your father these days. Swecha, Pragna, you both can't tolerate if anyone makes women suffer. Now I'll show you one thing."

As Lakshmi is sleeping, he takes both of his daughters to another place.

***

It is their old home;

They enter the home. He shows the photographs of 'Late Pragna' which were fixed to the wall in the living room.

Achyut: "She is your elder sister, 'Pragna'", he says by showing the first photograph which was captured during her first year.

Upon hearing his words, they both get shocked. He explains how they spent their time with her in that house, how they loved her and he shares with them every memory of her that is wandering in those rooms. Finally, he shows them the photograph of 'Late Pragna' which was captured during her 8th year.

Achyut: "It was her last picture!"

Pragna: "Last picture!!! What happened to her?", she exclaims doubtfully with fear.

He then opens a shelf and takes out an old newspaper and gives it to them.

Achyut: "Read that news!"

"An 8-year-old girl was brutally raped and murdered!", stated by the newspaper. They read the entire news.

Achyut: "The 8-year-old girl was your elder sister, Pragna!"

On hearing his words, they both turned to stone.

***

He then immediately takes them to the spot where Pragna was murdered.

"It happened a long ago, but you are feeling sad even now just by hearing it. But, just assume our pain as parents.", he says with a shivering tone.

"I found my beloved daughter dead when I came here to see her. We were almost dead when we saw your lifeless sister. But, we were born again when both of you were born to us.

"It is very important to be careful, if you want to make our lives beautiful. We shouldn't allow others to ruin our lives. Everyone has the right to live. No one has the right to kill the rights of others. If anyone tries to do so, you should oppose it, you should fight against them and you should fight for your rights!", he explains to them with razzle.

"To make you stubborn and fearless, I changed the place, I changed my attitude, I changed my behaviour towards my children and I did everything to make you learn everything. I want to see my girls as warriors!", he adds.

Swecha and Pragna hug their father.

Pragna: "We promise you dad!"

Swecha: "You believe and we will become!"

Pragna: "Yes, there is a need for freedom in this independent India!"

Swecha: "And we will show the way to that freedom!"

They took the pledge at that spot and left the place with determined minds.

***

CHAPTER 3

Few days later;

They completed their primary education and started their college life, another new phase of their lives.

One day in the college, during break time,

Swecha is alone in the classroom and writing some notes. At that moment, Vikram (her friend from school days) enters the classroom and sits in front of Swecha. Swecha looks at him, smiles and continues with her work. Vikram also smiles.

He looks nervous. He is trying to tell her something, but he is struggling inside to bring it out. Meanwhile, again she looks at him.

Swecha: "What?" she asks him casually.

Vikram: "I want to…"

Swecha: "You want to…?"

Vikram: "I Love you Swecha!"

Swecha: "You don't know whether I'm Swecha or Pragna, do you love me?" she laughs at him.

Vikram: "I know that you are Swecha!"

Swecha: "How can you say that?" she smiles.

Vikram: "There is a birthmark just below your nose, the little finger of your right hand has a scar on it, maybe it was an injury during your childhood, you don't like sports much but Pragna does. You are stubborn but very patient whereas she is an angry bird. Both are kind and never mind unnecessary things. See, to love you, I had to know about both of you. Maybe you both were born similar but you are entirely different.", he explains everything to her.

Swecha: "Good! Everything is right except the names. Nice observation but failed in execution!", she laughs.

(till here, I mentioned her name as Swecha according to Vikram's perception)

By the time she says that, *Swecha* shouts from outside: "Pragna, come out, we are waiting…"

On hearing Swecha's voice, he poses a confused face and realizes that the girl who is sitting in front of him is Pragna.

Pragna: "So, you love me by observing our physical appearances and activities. Vikram, when you can recognize me without seeing the scar on my finger and the mark under my nose, then come to me. Until then, focus on your career.", she says to him gently and leaves the room.

He remains silent.

***

114

After the college, Pragna and Swecha go to a district library and collect some newspaper cuttings from the records and then return home.

***

On that night;

Both of them sit in the living room and take out the paper cuttings they brought. They are as follows…

News 1: On December 16, 2012, a 23-year-old female student was beaten and gang raped brutally by six men in a moving bus passing by a middle-class South Delhi neighbourhood. After the attack, they threw her out onto the roadside.

News 2: Shakti Mills gang-rape, July-August 2013

A 22-year-old photojournalist and her male colleague were attacked, and she was raped by five men, including a minor, on August 22 in an abandoned mill in Central Mumbai. The accused threatened her they would post her photos online if she complained. Another 18-year-old alleged being raped in the same premises on July 13 by the same gang.

News 3: Protests broke out in Bangalore after a six-year-old was allegedly raped by school staff at an international school, Vibgyor High.

News 4: Uber rape case, December 2014

A 27-year-old woman was raped by her driver in Delhi while she was returning home in an Uber cab after she dozed off in the backseat and woke up to find him molesting her. Threatening to kill her, the driver then thrashed and raped her inside the locked car.

News 5: An 8-year-old child was killed after rape in Mansaur on 27th June 2018.

News 6: On August 9, 2018, three men from Salalpur Marheen village raped an 8-year-old girl in Chabe Chak area of Rajbagh, Kathua district of Jammu and Kashmir.

The doctors who conducted a post-mortem on the rape victim told the court that the girl was sexually assaulted and she died of asphyxia, a lawyer has said.

There are many other such heart-wrenching cases they have seen in those paper cuttings.

Swecha: "What happened to our India!?" she exclaims upon reading them.

Pragna: "That means, there are humans in our country, humans in terms of appearance, but not in terms of behaviour!"

Swecha: "How they did to an 8-year-old kid? Did she wear a short dress or did she expose her cleavage or something? No courtesy, bloody barbarians!"

Achyut: "Being emotional is not the way Swecha. You know one thing, the 23-year-old girl who was brutally raped in a moving bus in Delhi fought for her life in the hospital for 12 days and died on the 13th day. On that same day you both were born here. That is 2012, and this is 2027. You are 15-year-old now. Justice served her on this last Friday, after fifteen long years!", he comes home from the office and expresses his anguish.

They both remain silent

Achyut: "So girls, explore all the ways and possibilities to initiate a greater change and to ignite the young India. Be the cause, the cause for a change, the change that renovates India!", he concludes.

***

Their father's words recurred in their minds throughout the night and prevented them from sleeping.

While they are going home, Swecha's cycle is punctured. So, they are walking along with their bicycles. "I'm not feeling well Swecha, I'll go, you come carefully", says Pragna after walking for sometime.

Swecha holds Pragna's hand and feels the temperature and says "Hey! Can you ride a bicycle? Or I'll ride it, you sit back and we leave mine here somewhere."

"No Swecha, it is better to ride than sitting at the back. I'll go, no problem.", Pragna replies and goes from there.

***

Swecha then slowly comes to the puncture shop, and the guy is examining the tube.

Meanwhile, a girl is waiting for the city bus at the bus stop which is a few feet away from the puncture shop. A car stops in front of her. The man in the car downs the mirror and starts talking with that girl. It looks like she doesn't like talking to him. Swecha notices it and starts observing them. He is pointing the finger and threatening her and she is pleading with him to leave her. But, after a few minutes she gets into the car and the car leaves the place.

Here, the guy is still repairing her bicycle. Another guy who is repairing a bike from a while ago, makes it ready to go. She then takes the bike without saying a word and starts chasing the car.

While she is chasing the car, she notices a policeman who is beating someone at the roadside. She then stops the bike at some distance from them and says in a provoking manner, "Hey! You the inefficient inspector, I've no license and helmet. Instead of beating him, catch me right now if you have guts!" and starts again.

The angry inspector along with the person and constables starts chasing her on the jeep. She is chasing the car and the inspector chasing her.

Finally, the car reaches a godown. The man and the girl get down from the car. By the time Swecha reaches there, another man who is already waiting outside the godown pours acid on that girl's face. She screams in pain and falls to the ground. She gets choked and dies on the spot.

Swecha is greatly shocked on seeing it. All her efforts to save her went in vain. Even the policemen who came there by following her saw the incident. It's all happened in a split second. Even the men who didn't notice her following them get shocked to see them.

Swecha grabs his collar forcefully and shouts at him "why did you do this?"

The inspector then tries to pull Swecha back and the constables catch the two men.

"Sir, I deliberately provoked you to save that girl. I got suspicious when he was talking to that girl at the bus stop itself. That's why I followed them. But, this monster killed her brutally in front of us, we failed to save her. Kill him right now sir, kill him right now!" Swecha screams at the inspector with grief.

"Okay, he will be punished, you please calm down!" the inspector tries to calm her down and orders one constable to drop her at her home.

"Sir! Call me for the evidence whenever needed with no hesitation. I'll come!", she says to him before leaving the place.

***

The Next day;

Swecha searches the newspaper in the morning. There is the news regarding the acid attack on the girl. But the guy in the picture is not the one who she saw yesterday. She then rushes to the police station.

***

At the Police station;

Swecha questions the inspector about the changed picture in the news.

"Listen, he is the son of an MP, so they managed everything. He who is in the picture is a regular pick-pocketer. There is pressure from our higher officials to leave him. And it is not at all safe for you to come like this. If they come to know the girl who followed him is you, they will kill you!" the inspector says.

"Are you threatening me?" she questions him.

"I'm suggesting you protect yourself," he replies.

"Can you suggest yourself to do the same, if this happened to your daughter?" she asks him.

123

"You are crossing your limits!" he says with a raising tone.

"You are forgetting your duty, shame on you sir!" she says with anger and leaves the station.

***

In the college;

Swecha and Pragna are in the class. But Achyut's (father) words recurring in Swecha's mind: "the 23-year-old girl who was brutally raped in a moving bus in Delhi, that is 2012 and this is 2027, but still there is no proper justice served to her!"

"Being emotional is not the way Swecha, explore all the ways and possibilities to initiate a greater change and to ignite the young India. Be the cause, the cause for a change, the change that renovates India!"

***

Later they go to the chemistry lab for practice sessions. There, with the knowledge gained from the lecturers and by applying her intelligence, Swecha prepares a powerful acid. She then seals it in a bottle and keeps it in her bag carefully when no one observes her.

***

While they are on the way to their home after the college, traffic is jammed at a junction as some people are carrying a dead body for cremation. Suddenly the cloth on the face is slightly disturbed by wind. She is the girl who died because of acid attack. People at the junction turn their heads and are embarrassed to see her burnt face. Some of her friends are following her by holding small boards with the slogans on them: "stop acid attacks!" "stop violence against women!"

Swecha then covers the cloth on her face. On the opposite side, the guy who poured acid is in a car. Swecha notices him. She then takes out the acid bottle from her bag and grabs a helmet from a person. She fastly approaches his car, breaks the window mirror with the helmet, unlocks the door, holds his collar and drags him out of the car.

"Tell the people you are the one who killed her brutally. If not, I'll pour this acid on you!" she threatens him by showing the acid bottle in her other hand.

Instead of telling the truth, he tries to pour the same acid on her.

But before he does that, she pours it on him and says "Now the justice has served!"

He gets choked and dies on the spot.

The very daring and bold act of Swecha throws everyone into shock and silence.

"We know that those Police officers changed the person, but we kept silent as we have no strength to fight against them and we are stricken by grief. But, you did justice to my child. Now my child will rest in peace!" the girl's father, Swamy says, breaking the silence.

"Every girl should have at least half of your courage and guts. Then no one can dare to mess with a girl! You go my child, you did this for us and now it's our responsibility to protect you. Not only police, even we know how to change the persons and evidence." he says by taking the acid bottle into his hands.

"Uncle, but this is not...." She tries to tell something.

"We want people like you to be with us and among us, so please!" he requests her.

"Yes! Please be with us!" everyone requests her.

Upon listening to all their words, she decides to do so.

***

Later, policemen arrest Swamy after he performs last rites for his daughter. But because of the fierce opposition from

127

the public, the police department accepts the truth: due to the misleading of some of their personnel, they arrested Raju (pick-pocketer) in lieu of Stephen (MP's son). Also, they reduce Swamy's sentence from life to five years.

At the public's request, Swecha's family moves from that old isolated village to the city to live a safe and secure life.

***

CHAPTER 4

After Few Years...

Bubbles Pub; Hyderabad; 11:10PM IST;

Some boys and girls are dancing together and celebrating their friend's birthday. Most of the girls take alcohol beyond the permissible level and lose their control. Suddenly someone stops the music.

"Who is it?" one girl shouts by looking into the darkness.

"Pragna I.P.S.", the voice comes from the darkness and when someone turns on the lights, they see Pragna standing in front of them.

"What happened mam? Why are you disturbing us?" a boy questions her.

She then slaps him and says, "Late night parties, students like you consuming alcohol, drugs and all these extra-curricular activities are strictly prohibited in my city. Those who breach these rules should be punished. So, you all are under arrest!"

"This is ridiculous! You shouldn't arrest us, we all are from MP's and MLA's families and I'm the son of MLA Bucchibabu.", the birthday boy opposes her statement.

Pragna slaps him too and says, "Learn to tell your name first, not your father's name!"

***

At Cyber Towers; Hyderabad; 7:00 AM IST;

Pragna sits on the police jeep. A lengthy line of twenty to thirty cars are parked on the side of the road. Many big shots and other influential people in the city including few women assemble there in front of Pragna. And their children are watching the LIVE in their respective homes.

"Why did you arrest our children?"

"you are crossing your limits!"

"it is better to concentrate on other big criminals instead of arresting students for silly reasons!"

"you are curbing their freedom!"

"you are wasting our precious time!"

In this way, they raise different questions and oppose her action.

"Someone said I'm crossing limits. I'm not crossing limits, in fact your children are. Wearing lesser clothes and being closer to more than one person. Can you call this as being in limits? Can you take it as normal? But I can't!

"I'm not curbing their freedom, they are misusing their freedom. Most of the children who are least supervised or monitored will become big criminals in the future and no matter whether they came from the lower class or the higher class.

"The majority of India's population is youth. Country's future is in our hands, so it is the responsibility of every young individual to live every second consciously and purposefully.

"And last but not least, spending some time to know about your children is more important than your meetings and all. So, it is all up to you my dear parents, I'm leaving this to your own intelligence. Your children have reached your homes safely. Go and meet them, bye!" she replies with a smile.

After listening to her words, they all disperse from there silently.

****

On that night;

A girl is running in a desolate place. Three men are chasing her from behind. Suddenly they stop, on seeing a sign board there. It mentions that the area is under CCTV Surveillance. But one of them ignores the board and crosses the pole. Then, a siren blows within no time. Upon hearing the siren, they try to escape from that place, but some guys surround them with guns in their hands.

****

They throw the three men into the cell.

Pragna approaches the cell and says, "Each and every inch of this city is under Pragna's surveillance. I have many eyes. We know all the places you don't even know!"

"Thank you so much Ma'am! You saved my life!" the girl says from behind.

"That's okay! But, see my dear, we must run for our dreams, but not to escape from others. Make the habit of fighting instead of running!" Pragna advises her.

"Sure mam, I'll", she replies.

"You can!" Pragna says to her and asks one of the lady constables to drop her at her home.

After sometime, Pragna too reaches her home.

***

Her mother, Lakshmi opens the door.

"Oh, my dear mother! How many times, I told you not to wait for me.", Pragna asks her mother while removing her shoes.

"There is nothing wrong with waiting for my daughter. Also, you both are the heroes of the city.", Lakshmi replies.

"Dad made us heroes, and you extended your support for us to continue being heroes. If you don't stand behind us as an MLA, our job may become tougher. Now, no one questions us because of you."

"No Pragna! You both are honest. Honesty and truth must be accepted this way or the other way. And I'm not supporting my daughters, I'm supporting the good cause, I'm supporting the change and I'm supporting the truth!" she replies proudly with a smile.

***

After the dinner, Pragna makes a call to Swecha. Swecha is living somewhere in a small house. She lifts the call.

Swecha: "Hello, my dear sister! How are you and how's the city?"

Pragna: "Yeah! Me and our city are fine!"

Swecha: "So, is there any change in public opinion?"

Pragna: "Still, there is some opposition, but that's okay, this day or other day, they will understand our intention!"

Swecha: "Yes! That's true. And what about safety measures regarding women"

Pragna: "No worries Swecha, all our plans are getting executed well. The attacks on women are drastically reduced. Our mission to renovate freedom in our country becomes successful in four cities so far! You are doing a marvellous job as an undercover cop. Let's continue our good work and you, especially concentrate on growing the team!"

Swecha: "Of course we will and we can! By the way, it's been three weeks now, we have switched our roles. When again?" she laughs.

Pragna: "Well, next week I'll take the charge as an undercover cop, so you then come to the city then." she replies and laughs.

***

It will continue….

***

Later, one day, Pragna meets the Chief Minister and requests him to conduct personal development and karate classes for both the genders in all the schools and colleges as a part of their academics! And also to conduct awareness campaigns and workshops to all the parents along with their kids and teach them how to guide their children at their

137

different stages of life and how to be strong, conscious and brave in the times of difficulties and hazardous situations.

"We must conduct these awareness programs frequently at least thrice in a year, in all the parts of India from every small village to metropolitan cities.", Pragna requests the Chief Minister.

The chief minister then considers her request as a valuable suggestion which is helpful for the people to develop a healthy and positive mindset, to habituate a positive lifestyle and to live together in peace and harmony! Hence, he promised her to place this proposal in front of our Prime Minister and implement all these as soon as possible!

***

"Where the people accept and allow the change, where the people support a good cause, there we can see the happy and prosperous lives! Any change can be brought by collective efforts. If anyone takes the initiative, support him/her, give your efforts too if possible. That's the healthy sign.

"But most of us are habituated to drag others back who try honesty, genuinely and sincerely for bringing a change. This is the major reason why India has been a developing country for decades! First, accept this truth. Then the change comes automatically!"

--- Your Hemant Karicharla

Steps must be taken to eradicate such inhuman attacks on women:

To the Girls/Women:

• Education alone is not enough, you must know how to deal with such difficult and hazardous situations.

• You must be mentally strong first, then your brain sends you the message to fight, otherwise the same brain sends you the message to surrender.

To the Parents:

• Don't raise your girls as daughters, train them and make them as fighters.

• Try to teach them how to save themselves in such critical tricky conditions.

• Make them learn and make them aware of what is happening around them in the society.

• Discuss each and everything with them openly and freely without feeling shy or embarrassed.

• Tell them the difference between a friendly touch and a bad touch.

• Teach your sons how to respect and protect women.

To the Government:

• Software applications alone can't save her!

• Conduct awareness programs or workshops and train every girl in such a way that they must overcome fear and transform as brave hearts.

• Make these training programs or sessions mandatory in every city and every village to every girl.

- And such training programs, personal development classes must include in the curriculum of each and every school, colleges and university.

- Recruit special teams and appoint them at all the deserted places where there is a higher possibility of occurring such acts.

- Install secret cameras in such areas and monitor every activity taking place in those areas from control rooms. If you notice anything suspicious, immediately inform the special team who are at the particular place.

- If required, send a special force immediately to that place with no delay.

- And if possible, you can build a few police stations nearby such deserted places.

To the Judicial System:

• Punishments must be very strict. First, strike off the concept of forgiving. A death sentence must be the only action to be taken over such animals with no delay and with no second thought irrespective of the caste, cadre, religion, background etc etc…

• If and only if the laws are strict, then only the crime rate will be reduced.

Remember one thing, if he made a mistake, we can forgive him. But if he committed a sin, he must be punished!

***

"Women are not the puppets; they are creators and they are kingmakers! Don't mess with their patience, if their patience dies, then no one can save you from them. It's not a warning, it is the truth!"

Jai Hind!

Your Hemant